For those looking for their perfect home.

Original title: "Una casa per la famiglia Scoiattolo. Un curioso viaggio nell'architettura" © 2023 Franco Cosimo Panini Editore S.p.A., Modena

All rights in this publication are reserved to Franco Cosimo Panini Editore S.p.A. Nopart of this publication may be reproduced, stored in any retrieval system or transmitted in any form or by any means, electronic, mechanical, photocopying, recording or otherwise without the prior written permission of Franco Cosimo Panini Editore S.p.A. Published in agreement with Phileas Fogg Agency, Italy.

Photography credits:
Farnsworth House - Benjamin Lipsam/CC-BY-20
Capital Hill Residence - Zaha Hadid Architects Studio, London
Fallingwater - Sxenko/CC BY-3.0
Casa Batlló - FrDr/CC BY SA-4.0
Villa Savoye - Alessio Antonietti/CC BY-SA 3.0
Villa Vals ("The Hole") - Iwan Stöcklin/CC BY 4.0
Die Welt Steht Kopf - backkratze/CC BY 2.0
Gehry House - IK's World Trip/CC BY-2.0
Villa Almerico Capra ("La Rotonda") - Stefan Bauer/CC BY SA-2.5
Mushroom House of the Maggiolina District, Milan - Anonymous
Villa Malaparte - Nemo bis/CC BY SA-3.0

For the U.S. edition © Tra Publishing, 2025
Nuts About Architecture
A Home for the Squirrel Family
By Martina Tonello

Publisher and Creative Director
Ilona Oppenheim

Art Director
Jefferson Quintana

Editorial Director
Lisa McGuinness

Publishing Coordinator
Jessica Faroy

This product is made of FSC®-certified and other controlled material.
Tra Publishing is committed to sustainability in its materials and practices.

Printed and bound in China by Artron Art Co., Ltd.

ISBN: 978-1-9620981-5-1

Tra Publishing
245 NE 37th Street
Miami, FL 33137
trapublishing.com

T tra.publishing

1 2 3 4 5 6 7 8 9 10

Nuts about Architecture
A HOME FOR THE SQUIRREL FAMILY

MARTINA TONELLO

*Mr. and Mrs. Squirrel
live in a beautiful home.
It's exactly the way they want it to be:
small and simple, with a floor made of wood.*

*It's just the two of them. They love being close to nature,
and they don't need more space
to be happy.*

*But then...four baby squirrels arrived
and the family grew.
Now there are SO many toys!
Books.
Art supplies.
Rubber balls.
Tiny teacups.
Little flags.
Ropes for climbing.
A collection of stones.*

*And the house is DEFINITELY too small!
The time has come for the Squirrel family
to find a new home.*

You two are coming with me.

*So how do you find a new home?
Here's Mr. Raccoon, from the famous
Raccoon Real Estate Agency, coming to the rescue.
He's the BEST at finding the perfect solution
for all your real estate needs!*

We'd like a house filled with light, with a beautiful yard so that our little ones can enjoy themselves outside, and Mr. Squirrel and I can grow a small garden.

Welcome to the simplest, most modern home
you could possibly find in the woods!
All the walls are made of glass.
You will feel like you are living in the trees.
The Magpie family is selling it at
a very special price.
It seems they're in a BIG hurry to move...

We're actually moving TODAY.
We've found a more private home...
one more suited to our, ummm...
daily activities...

As the architect who designed this home said,
"Less is more," meaning: the less stuff you have around you, the better.
Here you can see a single large room.
From the living room you can go right into the kitchen,
and then to the bedroom.

Thanks to the glass walls,
the house is full of light.
You won't find another like it!

And the bathroom?
Here it is, smack in the middle of the house.
It's the only room with a door,
for obvious reasons!

Thank you, Mr. Raccoon.
This house is definitely...fascinating.
But there is too much glass to clean,
and we'd need another room for our kids.

I understand.
Don't worry,
I have another home to show you,
one that I believe will suit
all your needs!

You need a large space, but you don't want
a house that looks like all the others?
Here's a house that's truly one of a kind!
Its design is unique and it's surrounded by forest.
It's available to move in right away.
The movers are already here!

And then...if we take the elevator, we come to the bedrooms. They are more than seventy feet above the ground! You'll wake up each and every day to a clear blue sky!

This is truly original, Mr. Raccoon. But...it's much too large for us.

Not to worry! I have the PERFECT home for you!

Your family will gather around this warm fireplace.
It's absolutely beautiful!
It was excavated right into the surrounding
boulders, and it will make you feel
a part of nature!

You can enjoy this beautiful woodland setting without even having to leave the house. And you can take this stairway directly to the river.

It's truly stupendous, no doubt, Mr. Raccoon! But I think it'll be a bit too damp for us Squirrels, and it's also too far from the city.

Well...hmm...I have the perfect solution for you. Follow me!

Here we have a city home, completely renovated in the most spectacular way! And the current owner is joining us on our tour.

You'll love it here. We're selling it to be closer to the water. Actually...to be IN the sea!

Isn't it fantastic?
The front looks like waves, and the colors are like the beach.

And here we are on the main floor. This is the Grand Salon, with gorgeous stained-glass windows!

Here's a unique mushroom-shaped fireplace...

and a beautiful skylight that spreads light everywhere.

—This one? —It would make us dizzy!

—This one? —Too weird!

—Too formal.

—Too mushroomy.

You're a hard to please family,
I realize that now, but I have
ONE more house to show you!
First, I'd like to take you to the rooftop.
After climbing this staircase,
you'll have a view that will
take your breath away.
You're going to fall in love with it!

Here, you can marvel at nature's sheer power.
Would you like to see the inside now?

And although this home is truly fascinating, the sea wouldn't feel like home for us.

Mr. Raccoon, will we ever find a home that's just right for us?

Errr...at the moment, I don't have anything else to show you. But we can head back to the office to check if any new sale offers have come in.

Right this way.

Hey...what about THAT one?

This is IT!
It's perfect!
It's our new home!

Umm, okay... maybe with some remodeling?

FOR SALE AS IS

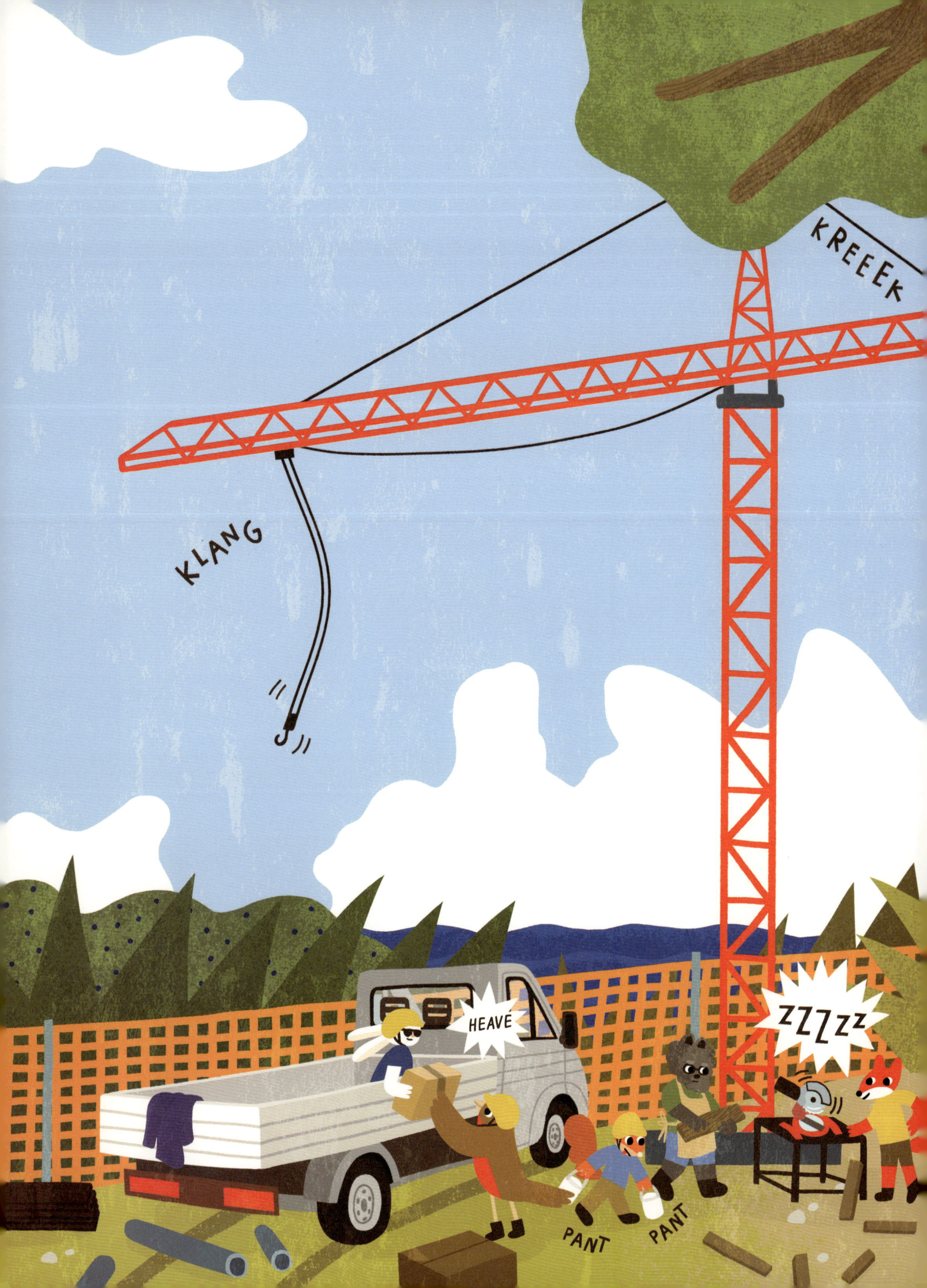
KREEEK
KLANG
HEAVE
ZZZZZ
PANT
PANT

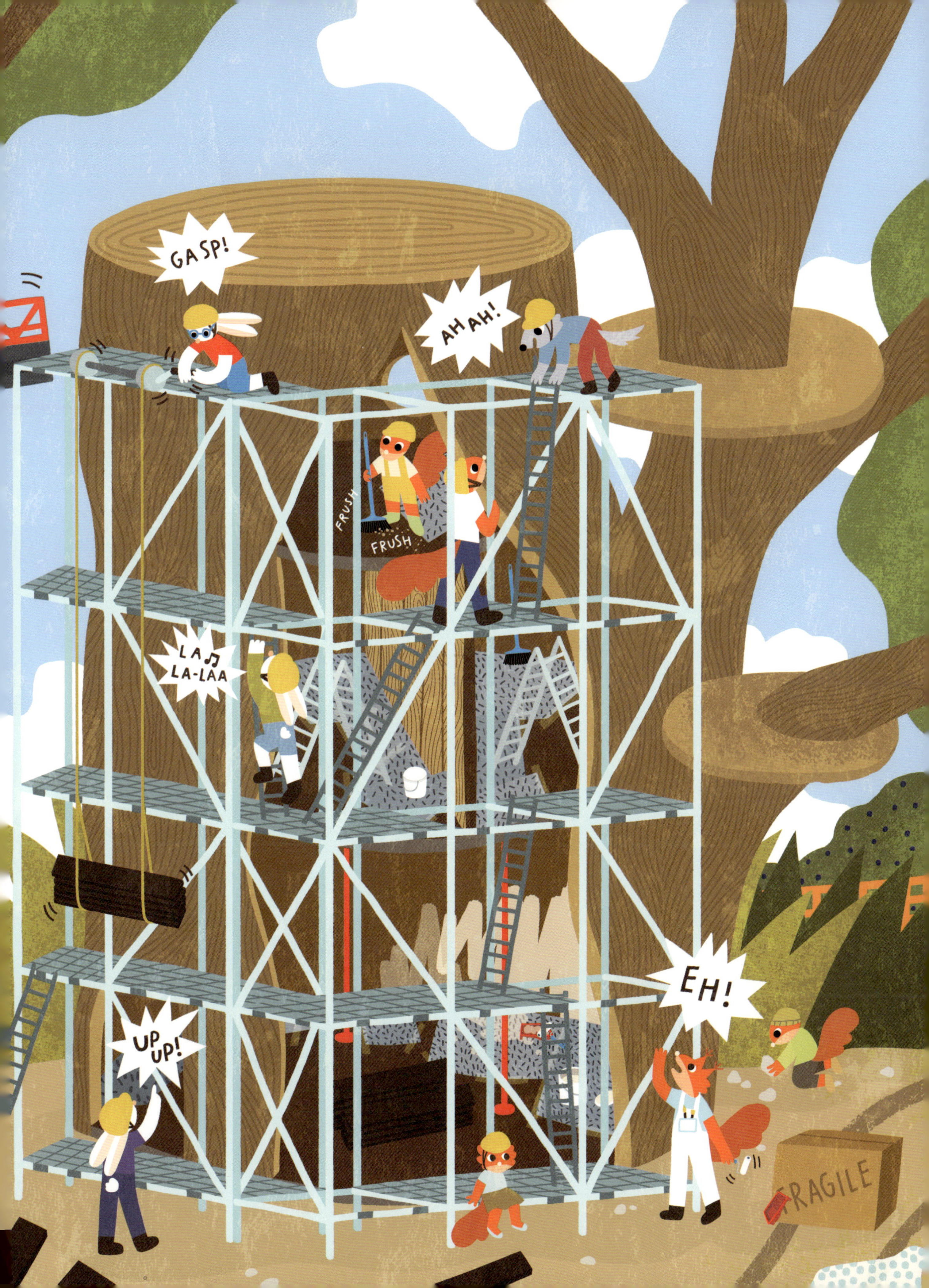
GASP!
AH AH!
FRUSH
FRUSH
LA LA-LAA
EH!
UP UP!
FRAGILE

After some renovations,
the Squirrel family's home was
ready to welcome them!
Carved out of a hollow tree trunk, it is
three very light-filled stories tall,
with two bedrooms, a study,
many balconies, a huge yard, and a garden.
There's even a little tree house!

It suits its owners perfectly,
and there's room for all their things:
toys, books, art supplies,
rubber balls, tiny teacups,
little flags, ropes for climbing,
a collection of stones...
and many new adventures.

RACCOON REAL ESTATE

FOR SALE

FARNSWORTH HOUSE
Designed by Ludwig Mies van der Rohe
1945-1951. Plano, Illinois (USA)

CAPITAL HILL RESIDENCE
Designed by Zaha Hadid
2006-2018. Barvikha, Moscow (Russia)

SPECIAL OFFER!

FALLINGWATER
Designed by Frank Lloyd Wright
1935-1939. Mill Run, Pennsylvania (USA)

INCREDIBLE!

CASA BATLLÓ
Designed by Antoni Gaudí
Renovated 1904-1906. Barcelona (Spain)

IDEAL!

VILLA SAVOYE
Designed by Le Courbusier
Built between 1928-1930. Poissy (France)

VILLA VALS, A.K.A. "THE HOLE"
Designed by Bjarne Mastenbroek and Christian Müller
Completed in 2009. Vals (Switzerland)

AGENCY

DIE WELT STEHT KOPF
Designed by Klaudiusz Golos and Sebastian Mikiciuk
Completed in 2008. Trassenheide (Germany)

GEHRY HOUSE
Designed by Frank Gehry
Completed in 1978. Santa Monica, California (USA)

RENOVATED!

VILLA ALMERICO CAPRA,
A.K.A. "LA ROTONDA" (THE ROUND ONE)
Designed by Andrea Palladio.
Built between 1567-1605. Vicenza (Italy)

PERFECT!

MUSHROOM HOUSE OF THE MAGGIOLINA DISTRICT
Designed by Mario Cavallé
Completed in 1946. Milan (Italy)

GREAT OFFER

VILLA MALAPARTE
Designed by Adalberto Libera
Completed in 1943. Capri (Italy)

SOLD!

SQUIRREL HOUSE
Designed by Martina Tonello
Renovated between 2022-2023. Monzuno (Italy)